... dinosaur ... he's an **ASTROSAUR!** Captain of the amazing spaceship DSS *Sauropod*, he goes on dangerous missions and ... cr... ...d Iggy.

For more astro-fun visit the website
www.astrosaurs.co.uk

Read all the adventures of
Teggs, Gipsy, Arx and Iggy!

RIDDLE OF THE RAPTORS

THE HATCHING HORROR

THE SEAS OF ████████

THE MIND-SWAP M█████

THE SKIES OF FEAR

THE SPACE GHOSTS

DAY OF THE DINO-DROIDS

THE TERROR-BIRD TRAP

TEETH OF THE T.REX
(specially published for
World Book Day 2007)

THE STAR PIRATES

THE CLAWS OF CHRISTMAS

THE SUN-SNATCHERS

Read all the adventures of Teggs, Blink
and Dutch at Astrosaurs Academy!

DESTINATION: DANGER!
CONTEST CARNAGE!
TERROR UNDERGROUND!

Find out more at www.astrosaurs.co.uk

Astrosaurs

REVENGE OF THE FANG

ALVA
ACADEMY

Steve Cole

Illustrated by Woody Fox

RED FOX

REVENGE OF THE FANG
A RED FOX BOOK 978 1 862 30255 6

First published in Great Britain by Red Fox,
an imprint of Random House Children's Books
A Random House Group Company

This edition published 2008

1 3 5 7 9 10 8 6 4 2

Text copyright © Steve Cole, 2008
Cover illustration and cards © Dynamo Design, 2008
Map © Charlie Fowkes, 2008
Illustrations copyright © Woody Fox, 2008

The right of Steve Cole to be identified as the author of this work
has been asserted in accordance with the Copyright, Designs and
Patents Act 1988.

The Random House Group Limited supports the Forest Stewardship
Council (FSC), the leading international forest certification organization.
All our titles that are printed on Greenpeace-approved FSC-certified paper
carry the FSC logo. Our paper procurement policy can be found at
www.rbooks.co.uk/environment.

Typeset in Bembo Schoolbook by Palimpsest Book Production Limited,
Grangemouth, Stirlingshire

Red Fox Books are published by Random House Children's Books,
61–63 Uxbridge Road, London W5 5SA

www.**kids**at**randomhouse**.co.uk
www.**rbooks**.co.uk

Addresses for companies within The Random House Group Limited can
be found at: www.randomhouse.co.uk/offices.htm

THE RANDOM HOUSE GROUP Limited Reg. No. 954009

A CIP catalogue record for this book is available from the British Library.

Printed in the UK by CPI Bookmarque, Croydon, CR0 4TD

To Oliver Meek,
lucky winner of the PBC competition

WARNING!

THINK YOU KNOW ABOUT DINOSAURS?

THINK AGAIN!

The dinosaurs . . .

Big, stupid, lumbering reptiles. Right?

All they did was eat, sleep and roar a bit. Right?

Died out millions of years ago when a big meteor struck the Earth. Right?

Wrong!

The dinosaurs weren't stupid. They may have had small brains, but they used them well. They had big thoughts and big dreams.

By the time the meteor hit, the last dinosaurs had already left Earth for ever. Some breeds had discovered how to travel through space as early as the Triassic period, and were already enjoying a new life among the stars. No one has found evidence of dinosaur technology yet. But the first fossil bones were only unearthed in 1822, and new finds are being made all the time.

The proof is out there, buried in the ground.

And the dinosaurs live on, way out in space, even now. They've settled down in a place they call the Jurassic Quadrant and over the last sixty-five million years they've gone on evolving.

The dinosaurs we'll be meeting are

 part of a special group called the Dinosaur Space Service. Their job is to explore space, to go on exciting missions and to fight evil and protect the innocent!

These heroic herbivores are not just dinosaurs.

They are *astrosaurs*!

NOTE: The following story has been translated from secret Dinosaur Space Service records. Earthling dinosaur names are used throughout, although some changes have been made for easy reading. There's even a guide to help you pronounce the dinosaur names on the next page.

Talking Dinosaur!

How to say the prehistoric
names in this book...

STEGOSAURUS – *STEG-oh-SORE-us*

HADROSAUR – *HAD-roh-sore*

DIPLODOCUS – *di-PLOH-de-kus*

PTEROSAUR – *teh-roh-SORE*

TRICERATOPS – *try-SERRA-tops*

IGUANODON – *ig-WA-noh-don*

OVIRAPTOR – *OHV-ih-RAP-tor*

DIMORPHODON – *die-MORF-oh-don*

BAROSAURUS – *bar-oh-SORE-us*

DICERATOPS – *dye-SERRA-tops*

THE CREW OF THE DSS SAUROPOD

**CAPTAIN
TEGGS STEGOSAUR**

ARX ORANO,
FIRST OFFICER

GIPSY SAURINE,
COMMUNICATIONS
OFFICER

IGGY TOOTH,
CHIEF ENGINEER

Jurassic Quadrant

Ankylos

Steggos

Diplox

INDEPENDENT
DINOSAUR
ALLIANCE

vegetarian
sector

Squawk
Major

DSS
UNION OF
PLANETS

PTEROSAURIA

Tri System

Corytho

Lambeos

Iguanos

Aqua Minor

Geldos Cluster

Teerex
Major

Olympus

TYRANNOSAUR
TERRITORIES

Baronia

**carnivore
sector**

Raptos

Planet Sixty

Asteroid Beta

THEROPOD EMPIRE

Megalos

Cryptos

Tartara

**vegmeat
zone**

(neutral space)

SEA REPTILE
SPACE

Pliosaur
Nurseries

Not to scale

REVENGE OF
THE FANG

Chapter One

A PARTY SURPRISE

"Great galaxies, I'm going to be late!" cried Captain Teggs Stegosaur, struggling to do up a big black bow tie. "Late for a *very* important date!"

Teggs was an eight-ton, orange-brown stegosaurus. Normally he wore the red uniform of an astrosaur in the Dinosaur Space Service, and whizzed about having far-flung

adventures in his amazing spaceship the *Sauropod*. But today, Teggs was squeezed into a smart black dinner suit and bright white shirt, and was looking in his bedroom mirror. For one day only, he was not fighting evil or protecting the innocent . . .

He was going to his space-school reunion!

"Let me help you there," said Gipsy

Saurine, her skilled hooves expertly fastening Teggs's bow tie. She was a hadrosaur with green and yellow stripes, in charge of the *Sauropod*'s communications. "It's only midday. What time does the party start?"

"Not till seven-thirty tonight," Teggs told her. "But I'm meeting some old friends first — Blink and Dutch. We went through Astrosaurs Academy together."

Gipsy glanced at a photo on Teggs's bedside table. It showed a much younger Teggs standing between a small, cheeky-looking diplodocus and a yellow pterosaur with a big, beaky grin.

Teggs smiled happilly. "Blink is the dino-bird — he's a top navigator these days. And Dutch is the long-necked one! He patrols the borders of Sea Reptile Space. We're all meeting up at Blink's holiday home on Asteroid Beta and then going on to the big reunion."

Gipsy noticed a pretty red dinosaur with two horns in the background of the picture, making bunny ears over Teggs's head. "Who's that?" she wondered.

"Oh, that's just Damona," said Teggs, rolling his eyes. "She was very bright and very brave — but also *very* annoying! I think she became a spaceship captain like me . . ." He grinned. "It will be fun to catch up with my old gang!"

Suddenly, there was a knock at the door — and a green triceratops stepped into Teggs's bedroom, carrying a large potted plant. It was Arx Orano, Teggs's super-smart second-in-command. "We are approaching Asteroid Beta, Captain," he said. "Oh, and here's that plant you wanted."

Gipsy frowned. "Is it a present for Blink and Dutch?"

"Nope," said Teggs, "it's my pre-party snack!" He bounded over to Arx and devoured the plant in a single, enormous gulp. "Mmm, tasty!" he licked his lips. Teggs wasn't just the bravest astrosaur alive – he was the hungriest too! "Thanks for that, Arx, and thank you for helping me get ready, Gipsy. Now I'd better be off."

7

Arx put down the pot and saluted. "We shall stay on patrol and pick you up when you call. Iggy will be your taxi driver – he is waiting for you in the shuttle bay."

Teggs smiled. Iggy Tooth was the *Sauropod*'s chief engineer. A cheery iguanodon, he was always tinkering with the ship and its shuttles. "Well, I shan't keep him waiting!" He strode off

towards the shuttle bay. "See you later, guys – call me if you have any problems."

"Just relax and have a lovely time," Gipsy called after him. "It's your first day off in a year!"

With a spring in his step, Teggs reached the bay in no time. Iggy was waiting in Shuttle Alpha. The air was already full of thick smoke from the ship's powerful dung-burners.

Iggy saluted. "Ready to go, Captain."

"Then let's fly!" cried Teggs, jumping on board.

The shuttle bay doors cranked open and they shot off into star-speckled space. "We should reach Asteroid Beta in three minutes," Iggy predicted.

Sure enough, a tiny potato-shaped planetoid soon showed on the scanner. A sleek spacecraft stood on the visitors' launch pad beside an ultra-modern holiday home.

"That's a cool ship," noted Iggy as he gently landed the shuttle. "A custom-built Dungmaster with mark-four engines!"

"Dutch got it years ago, I helped him choose it!" said Teggs, smiling as he jumped outside. "Thanks for the ride, Ig. Bye!"

The shuttle took off again with lots of noise and smoke. As the door to the house was already open, Teggs expected his friends to come out and greet him. But they didn't.

Maybe they didn't hear me arrive, Teggs thought. He crossed to the front door. "Hello?" he boomed. "Blink? Dutch? Are you there?"

But the whole house was completely quiet.

Teggs went inside to the living room – and gasped. The whole place had been smashed up! Tables lay in splinters, armchairs were overturned, there were dents in the ceiling and scratch marks on the wall. A heap of delicious-looking ferns lay scattered on the floor in a puddle of leaf dressing. But for once, Teggs wasn't hungry.

"Dutch would never leave good food uneaten," he muttered. "His appetite is almost as big as mine. And Blink is the tidiest person I know – he would *never* leave his house looking like this." Teggs straightened up with a worried frown. "I think something seriously bad has happened here . . ."

Then, as he crossed into the kitchen, Teggs saw a message on the wall, scrawled in blood-red ink. A chill travelled from the tips of his toes to the tops of his tail-spikes as he read what it said:

DEAR CAPTAIN TEGGS,
IF YOU WANT TO SEE YOUR FRIENDS **ALIVE**, COME TO PLANET TARTARA ALONE.
TELL NO ONE – **OR ELSE!**
the FANG

Chapter Two

ENEMIES REUNITED

Teggs stared at the note, and the bony plates along his back flushed deep red with anger. "If this 'Fang' has hurt my friends," he growled, "he'll need a good dentist by the time I'm through with him!"

The steaming-mad stegosaurus charged out of the house and prepared to call the *Sauropod* for a lift. But then he hesitated.

"Arx, Gipsy and Iggy will want to know why I'm going to Tartara," Teggs realized, thinking out loud. "They would do anything to help. But if the Fang finds out I told them, then Blink and Dutch's lives will be at risk." He sighed and put the communicator back in his pocket, feeling very lonely. "There's no one I can turn to. I'm stuck in this mess alone." Teggs crossed to Dutch's spaceship, full of determination. "But alone or not, I'll teach this finky Fang never to mess with an astrosaur!"

Once he had found his way to the control room, Teggs checked Tartara's location on the star charts. Then he fired up the ship's engines and went roaring off into space.

It took four
anxious hours to
reach Tartara. It
was a million
miles away
and not much
to look at —
dull grey and
covered in big
round craters.

Then, just as Teggs curled his long
tail around the brake rockets, a cold
voice hissed over the spaceship's
speakers: "Welcome, Captain Teggs.
Your friends are quite safe — so long as
you obey. Enter at once through the
secret tunnel."

"What secret tunnel?" Teggs
demanded. But then he saw a large
crater slide open to reveal a black hole
in the grey rock. Taking a deep breath,
Teggs took tight hold of the control
stick and steered inside . . .

The secret tunnel was narrow and winding. At last it opened out into a massive parking bay, lit by orange floodlights. Teggs quickly parked the spaceship and jumped out. The bay was freezing cold, and the smell of raw meat hung in the air. Teggs had braved many evil lairs in his time, but some sixth sense told him now that he had never been in greater danger.

"Well, here I am," he called. "Alone, just as you asked. Show yourself, Fang!"

"Very well . . ." The voice seemed to echo all around him. "*We* will."

"*We?*" said Teggs, puzzled.

"Fool!" rasped another sinister voice that sounded strangely familiar. "FANG stands for Fearsome Army of Nasty Geniuses!"

Then a gruffer voice joined in: "Let's show the stego-scumbag who he's up against . . ."

A hidden door in the wall slid open. Teggs stared in amazement as a woolly mammoth with no tusks and a yellow hard hat barged into the bay. His trunk was wrapped around a small cement shooter, and his eyes glinted with menace.

Teggs gulped. "Uh-oh."

"Remember me, Captain?" the mammoth snarled.

Teggs thrust his chin out and stepped forward bravely. "Unfortunately, yes! You're Tonka — mammoth builder and sinister schemer. You once tried to smash up an entire planet just to make a bit of cash!"

"A brilliant plan," agreed Tonka. "But you spoiled it."

"He spoiled *my* plans too!" A mean little dinosaur with the eyes of a goblin and the teeth of a killer shark scuttled out from under Tonka's hairy tummy.

"It – it can't be!" Teggs's jaw dropped. "Crool Dasta, the evil inventor!"

"The same! My inventions would have made me mega-rich if you hadn't got in the way." Dasta snapped his teeth together. "And now we have plans for you, Teggs . . ."

"Let's forget our plans and squash him now!" rumbled Tonka. He aimed his cement shooter straight at Teggs. He couldn't miss!

But suddenly, a rasping voice rang out: *"Don't be a fool, Tonka!"* A chunky green dinosaur wearing shades and tight silver shorts burst into the room, and knocked the weapon aside.

Teggs knew his life had been saved, but his heart still sank faster than a stone in fern soup. "Oh, no," he whispered as the dinosaur stomped closer. "Not *you!*"

"Yes, Teggs." The dinosaur showed his pointed flesh-tearing teeth in a scary smile. "Attila the Atrocious is on the team too!"

"Then I don't give much for your team's chances of promotion," declared Teggs, with a cockiness he didn't feel. "You blew it when you tried to take over the universe, Attila – your dumb robotic dino-droids were all destroyed."

"*You* are the dumb one, Teggs," Attila hissed. "You only beat the three of us before by pure luck. But now that we have joined together we are invincible!"

"Makes a change from being *in prison*," said Teggs. "I thought you were all locked up. How did you get out?"

"*I* helped them," said a fourth voice, fierce and gurgling. The three villains parted to reveal an ugly, hunched-up raptor with a yellow crown and a royal red cape standing in the doorway. His beady eyes were fixed on Teggs.

"I'm having a nightmare!" Teggs cried. "This is impossible. It *can't* be you!"

"But it *is,* Teggs," hissed the horrible figure. "I, King Albu — egg-mad ruler of all oviraptors — have returned to make you pay as well!"

Teggs could only stare. "But I saw you eaten up by a hatching star-dragon ages ago!"

"Eaten?" For a moment King Albu looked baffled. "Pah! I am very much alive, as you can see."

"But how?" Teggs demanded.

"That's *my* secret," rasped the oviraptor. "I had to survive . .. so I could have my revenge on *you*!"

"We all want revenge," said Tonka, swinging his trunk menacingly.

"You must suffer as *we* have suffered!" hissed Crool Dasta.

"Yes," Attila cackled. "Suffer at the claws of the FANG!"

Teggs raised his eyebrows. "A fang with claws?"

Attila blushed as his fellow villains looked at him crossly. "You know what I mean!"

"I know you *are* mean. Extremely mean." Teggs marched boldly up to his four old enemies. "So, show me that my friends are safe!"

"Very well." Albu snapped his claw-like fingers, and Tonka the mammoth lumbered away through the door in the wall. He returned a few moments later herding Dutch the diplodocus and Blink the pterosaur ahead of him. Both were held helpless in heavy chains.

"Guys!" Teggs rushed up to them. "It's so cool to see you. Are you all right?"

"Just about, dude!" Dutch smiled bravely and knocked knuckles with Teggs. "Good to see you again . . . though it's not quite the party I was hoping for!"

"Teggs!" Blink attempted a small, fluttery somersault but the chains held him down.

"I'm sorry you were forced to come here." He wrapped the tip of his wing around Teggs's other hand and shook it firmly. "These villains burst into my holiday home and caught Dutch and me by surprise."

Dutch nodded. "We tried to fight but

they used knockout gas. We woke up here their prisoners."

"Wait." A nasty thought struck Teggs. "How do I know you're really *you* and not two of Attila's dino-droids?" Attila had fooled Teggs before with robot doubles of his closest friends. They had been perfect in every detail – and perfectly deadly.

"Your friends are flesh and blood, Captain," hissed Dasta. "Observe!" He flicked Dutch with a razor-sharp claw. Dutch gasped – and Teggs saw a red scratch appear.

"Would you like us to prove it again, Teggs?" Attila licked his lips. "I fancy a dino-snack!"

"Don't you dare try and hurt them!"

Teggs shouted. "Just tell me what this is all about."

"We have a job for you, Captain Teggs," gurgled King Albu. "We want you to steal a brand-new, top-secret invention – the only one of its kind in existence."

"It is being held in SSSS-One," Attila added, "the Super-Secure Space Station in sector seven."

"That's an astrosaur space station," Teggs realized. "The DSS own it."

"Indeed – which is why none of us can get anywhere near it," Dasta admitted. "But you, Teggs, can simply stroll in and help yourself!"

"Me, steal from the DSS?" Teggs went pale. "Give away vital secrets to the enemy?"

"That's right, Teggs," snarled Tonka. "Cos if you don't, your 'old friends' here won't be getting any older!"

"So I can only save Blink and Dutch

by becoming a traitor . . . ?" Teggs stared at him in horror. "Even if I win – I lose!"

"Precisely!" King Albu snarled as his evil friends shook with laughter. "And we shall have our revenge at last . . . The revenge of the FANG!"

Chapter Three

LIES AND SECRETS

Teggs racked his brain as his old
enemies hooted with laughter. He had
to find a way out of this miserable
mess. But how?

"Don't do what they want, dude,"
Dutch urged
him.

"We don't
matter,"
Blink added,
blinking
furiously.
"But top
DSS secrets
do!"

"Pah!" spat Crool Dasta. "You astrosaurs are so sickeningly brave!"

"And disgustingly loyal," Attila added, doing a little shimmy in his silver shorts.  "You would do anything to save your friends, Teggs – wouldn't you?"

"You know I would." Teggs's head drooped. "What *is* this invention you want me to steal?"

"It is called Mega-Spray Y," hissed King Albu.

"Y?" Teggs repeated.

"How should I know why!" the king gurgled. "But that is its name."

"If it's top secret, how did *you* find out about it?" Blink twittered.

Tonka smiled. "We have cracked the DSS's communications code. We can listen in to anything they say."

Dasta nodded. "And to be certain you do not try to double-cross us, Teggs, we shall bug you."

"You're already bugging me," growled Teggs.

Attila slapped a small metal disc on the stegosaur's shoulder under his dinner suit. "This device will transmit everything you say and do back to FANG HQ. If you ask for help or tell anyone about us, we shall destroy your friends at once."

"And don't think about trying to remove it,"

Dasta added. "It is booby-trapped. If you tug on it too hard, it will explode!"

Teggs gulped. "I always wanted to go out with a bang, but that's going too far!"

"Just shift, steg-breath," snapped Tonka. "It's time to start your criminal career!"

"You've got twelve hours to get back here with the Mega-Spray Y and save your friends." King Albu smiled nastily. "Some say revenge is a dish best served cold. But *I* say, revenge is a dish best served with poached eggs, lots of runny mashed potatoes and a large spoon!"

"That's because you're totally fruit-loops!" Teggs retorted. He saluted Blink and Dutch. "Don't worry, guys. Everything will work out fine, you'll see."

"Indeed it will," said Attila mockingly. "For *us*!"

★

Two hours later and just a few million miles away, the *Sauropod* was patrolling space. Arx sat in Teggs's control pit. Iggy and Gipsy stood at their stations, and the *Sauropod*'s pterosaur flight crew – fifty fast-flapping dimorphodon – pecked peacefully at their controls.

"I hope Captain Teggs is having fun," said Gipsy. "He never gets a chance to relax."

"Hang on." Arx had spotted something on the scanner screen. "Look at that little spaceship go!"

Iggy frowned. "That's the same ship I saw on Asteroid Beta when I dropped off Teggs. He said it belonged to his friend, Dutch."

"The Astrosaurs Academy reunion is in the opposite direction," Gipsy reminded him. "It can't be the same ship."

"But it *is*!" Iggy insisted. "A one-of-a-kind Dungmaster!"

"But why is it going so fast, and in

the wrong direction?" Arx jumped up. "Perhaps someone has stolen it!"

"I'll try to contact them," said Gipsy,

flicking some switches with her hooves. "This is the DSS *Sauropod* calling Dungmaster ship. Identify yourself, please." Then the astrosaurs gasped – as the image of Teggs appeared on the screen! He looked pale and tired.

"It's only me, Gipsy," said Teggs. "Dutch said I could borrow his ship."

"Captain? What's happening?" cried Arx. "We thought you would be having fun at the reunion by now – not zooming away from it."

"I . . ." Teggs sighed. "I couldn't go to the reunion."

"But why?" asked Gipsy.

Teggs wished he could tell his friends about the horrible things that had happened. But with the booby-trapped bug stuck to his  shoulder, the FANG would hear every word – and they would squish Blink and Dutch for sure! "Er . . ." He struggled to make something up. "Um, Admiral Rosso called to say he's got an urgent mission for me on SSSS-One."

Iggy frowned. "The Super-Secure Space Station in sector seven?"

"That's a pity," said Arx. "Still, if the admiral's involved it must be important. Shall we meet you there, Captain?"

"No, Arx," said Teggs quickly. "I'll handle this alone. Stay on patrol and I'll call when I can. Teggs out."

The astrosaurs watched their captain's face fade from the screen.

Arx raised his eyebrows. "I wonder what his mysterious mission can be?"

"Perhaps we'll find out," said Gipsy, holding a hoof to her headphones. "There's a call from Admiral Rosso coming through!"

She nodded to a dimorphodon, who banged a button with his beak. Rosso, the crusty old barosaurus in charge of the Dinosaur Space Service, appeared on the screen.

"Oh, hello, Arx," he said with a smile. "I'd like to have a quick word with Teggs. Where is he?"

Arx gave him a puzzled frown. "But surely you know he's not on board, sir? You've only just sent him on an urgent mission to SSSS-One."

"I most certainly have not!" Rosso retorted. "You must be mistaken."

"But Captain Teggs told us so just a few moments ago, Admiral," said Gipsy. "He's on his way there right now in a borrowed spaceship."

Iggy looked uneasily at Arx. "Maybe someone's playing a trick on him."

"Or perhaps he's in some sort of trouble," said Arx.

"If SSSS-One is involved we can't take any chances," said Rosso gravely.

"The Vegetarian Sector's most secret inventions are stored there! Get after Teggs and find out what's going on."

"Right away, Admiral," said Arx as the ever-eager dimorphodon rushed to their controls. "Let's get moving!"

Seconds later, the *Sauropod* was speeding away towards the space station.

Little did the astrosaurs know that, far away on Tartara, the four foul FANG members had used their communications-code-cracker to listen in on Rosso's conversation.

"So . . ." King Albu's cold hiss filled the FANG's control room. "The *Sauropod*'s crew think they can help Teggs, do they?"

"*No one* can help him!" roared Attila the Atrocious. He stamped over to where Blink and Dutch sat helplessly in the grotty cell next door and did a devilish disco wiggle. "For if Teggs does not return to us swiftly with the Mega-Spray Y. . . he and his friends will *DIE!*"

Chapter Four

THE SECRET SNATCHER

Teggs parked his borrowed spaceship and hurried aboard SSSS-One. His special all-access astrosaur "Captain's Card" allowed him to go almost anywhere on DSS property, and so far

no one on board had stopped to ask
him why he was visiting the Super-
Secure Space Station – nor why he
was dressed in a dinner suit. As he
galloped off to the Secret Inventions
storehouse, he hoped it stayed that
way.

He had just seven hours left to
get the Mega-Spray Y back to the
FANG HQ.

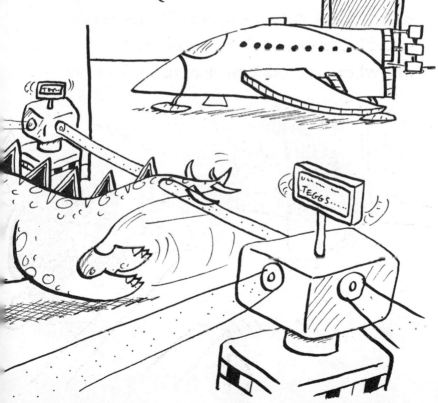

The storehouse had one of the biggest, thickest doors that Teggs had ever seen. It was made of ultra-tough metal and covered in huge locks. "No one can get in there without written permission from Admiral Rosso." Teggs sighed. "Oh, well. I'll have to try knocking . . ."

Steeling himself, he took a run-up, curled himself into a large, spiky bundle — and launched himself at the storehouse door at top speed. Over and over he went, like a giant self-propelled bowling ball, until — *KER-KLANNG!* He crashed headfirst into the heavy door and smashed it off its huge hinges!

At once, sirens went off and warning
red lights began to flash. Rubbing his
bruised head, Teggs hunted through row
after row of metal cabinets for the
Mega-Spray Y. Everything was in

alphabetical
order so it
didn't take
him long
to find the
right one.
Perhaps I can
pay for the
damages later,
Teggs thought hopefully. With a well-
aimed whack of his tail, he buckled the
door to the "M" cabinet and wrenched
it open. The only thing inside was a
small white case. Teggs snatched it up
and sprinted for the exit.

But a thick metal barrier was sliding
down over the doorway like a castle's
portcullis, ready to trap him inside.

"They don't call this place super-secure for nothing!" cried Teggs. Desperately, he slid along the floor on his tummy and just made it through the dwindling gap before the barrier closed.

But before Teggs could get up again, he saw ten ankylosaur security guards charging down the corridor, pointing pistols straight at him. Their scaly faces creased in confusion.

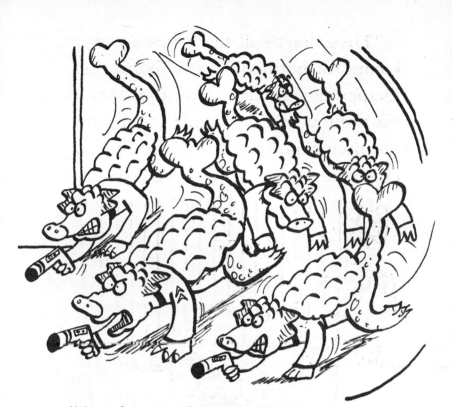

"Aren't you Captain Teggs
Stegosaur?" asked one of the guards.

"Yes, and I managed to stop some
thieves taking this case," Teggs panted,
pointing down the corridor with his
tail. "They went that way. Get after
them, quick!"

As the security guards ran off, Teggs
sighed. This was the worst day of his

47

life. He hated tricking good astrosaurs. But he knew there was no other way.

With the sirens still wailing wildly, Teggs hurried back towards the spaceship bay with the stolen case, his heart pounding like mad. The maze of corridors was a blur as he ran. "Not far now . . ." he told himself.

But as Teggs turned the final corner, he got a shock. Gipsy, Arx and Iggy were blocking the way ahead of him!

"Captain, what's going on?" Arx looked puzzled. "You told us Admiral Rosso sent you here — but he didn't."

Iggy pointed to the case. "And where are you taking *that* in such a hurry?"

Teggs longed to tell them the truth. But he remembered the bugging device under his dinner suit, and Attila's parting words: *If you ask for help or tell anyone about us, we shall destroy your friends at once* . . .

"Well, sir?" Iggy prompted him.

"It's . . . er . . ." Teggs gulped. "It's my packed lunch."

Gipsy frowned. "Then why does it say 'TOP SECRET INVENTION' in red letters on the side?"

"Captain!" Arx looked horrified. "I don't believe it. You — you can't be *stealing* . . . ?"

Behind him, over the sirens' scream, Teggs could hear the pounding of heavy feet. The security guards were coming! "Guys, let me pass," he snapped. "That's an order!"

Gipsy started walking towards him. "We are your friends," she said. "If you're in trouble, we want to help."

"Then stand aside," said Teggs, checking his watch – he had only six and a half hours to get the Mega-Spray Y back to Tartara. "I can't be caught now!"

"Someone's *making* you steal that thing," said Iggy hopefully. "Right, Captain?"

Teggs took a deep breath. "No more talk, guys. It's time to go!" With that, he tried to push past his friends – but Iggy and Gipsy grabbed hold of him. Desperately, he shook them free. They crashed against the walls, looking stunned and dismayed, and Teggs felt terrible.

"I – I'm sorry!" he told them.

"Captain, have you gone space crazy?" Arx thundered. He reared up and shoved Teggs backwards.

"I don't want to fight you, Arx," cried Teggs. "Get out of my way!"

"I can't," Arx shouted back. "An astrosaur upholds the law, he doesn't break it!"

Teggs glanced wildly back at Gipsy and Iggy. They were already getting to their feet behind him. And any moment now the security guards would appear round the corner . . .

"Please, Arx!" Teggs urged his old friend.

"No, Captain." Arx lowered his head, ready to charge. "If you want to escape . . . you'll have to get through me first!"

Chapter Five

WANTED! – TEGGS STEGOSAUR

"Forgive me, Arx," said Teggs miserably. "But I have no choice!"

He hooked one of his tail-spikes behind Arx's head-frill and yanked him forward with all his strength. The triceratops went tumbling into Iggy and Gipsy and the approaching guards, and they all went down in a scaly heap.

"Some day you'll understand," Teggs
told them, wiping a tear from his eye.
"I hope!" Then he dashed off again
towards the spaceship bay. He charged
headlong through still more guards,
scattering them like skittles, until finally
he reached Dutch's Dungmaster.

For a moment, Teggs looked longingly at the *Sauropod* parked nearby. "I'll get back to you," he swore. "I'll make things right, somehow."

Then he climbed aboard his borrowed ship, fired up the engines and used a DSS priority code to open the space station's outer doors. Moments later, he shot off into the endless starry night.

Teggs stared at the scanner, watching for the DSS ships he knew would be streaking to the scene and planning how to avoid them. He was a fugitive now, running not just for his own life – but for Blink's and Dutch's too . . .

★

Arx, Gipsy and Iggy ran back to the *Sauropod* with heavy hearts.

"I just can't believe the captain would turn into a crook!" Iggy exclaimed.

"*I* can't believe he just chucked us aside like that." Gipsy sighed. "What did he mean, 'Some day you'll understand'?"

Arx kept a stiff upper horn. "We must tell Admiral Rosso," he declared.

But as they entered the flight deck, they found the dimorphodon flapping

 about in alarm – and Admiral Rosso's frowning face already on the scanner screen.

"I've just been shown pictures from SSSS-One's security cameras," said Rosso gravely. "They clearly show Teggs stealing an invention. Look."

Rosso's face was replaced by a film of Teggs smashing down the storehouse door and rummaging about inside. Gipsy turned away, unable to watch, and Iggy gave her a comforting pat on the shoulder.

"We are trying to find out precisely which invention Teggs has stolen," said Rosso, reappearing on the screen. "In the meantime, he must be captured and made to explain himself. I am sending all available ships after him – including you." His head bobbed closer. "So get going!"

The screen went dark, and the astrosaurs walked slowly to their places.

Iggy shook his head. "Our own captain, a wanted dinosaur!"

"There *must* be more to this than

meets the eye," said Arx fiercely. "Teggs wouldn't give up on us if we were in trouble. So we must not give up on him."

Gipsy forced a smile and nodded. "Let's find him — and fast!"

Thousands of miles away, Teggs was roaring through space towards the FANG HQ on Tartara when the ship's computer piped up.

"Warning!" it stated. "Super-Secure Space Station-One has launched pursuit probes."

"Oh, no," groaned Teggs. Pursuit probes were like electronic guard dogs.

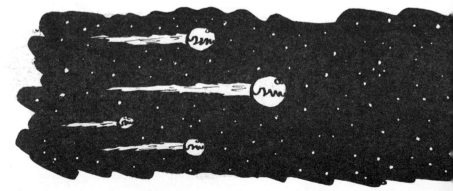

They flew through space, large, round and bristling with every weapon you could imagine. Once their sensors caught the scent of a spaceship's exhaust, they would never stop following. "Set speed to maximum," he said.

"It already *is* at maximum," the computer told him.

"Then make it maximum-plus-a-bit-more!" Teggs urged it.

"Impossible," said the computer.

Teggs sighed. If only Iggy were here, he would have the engines going faster in no time. He missed his fine ship and his brave crew. Once Blink and Dutch were safe, he would find a way to make the FANG pay for what they had done . . .

"Pursuit probes are gaining on us," said the computer calmly.

"*HALT!*" A mechanical voice grated over the ship's speakers. "This is Pursuit Probe One. Surrender or I shall open fire."

"I would if I could but I can't!" Teggs cried. "Computer, can we fire back?"

"The ship is unarmed," replied the computer.

"Then give me manual control!" Teggs took the giant joystick in both hands and steered sharply to the left. Then he looped the loop and sent

the ship shooting upwards. He *had* to
get away . . .

But suddenly, the ship lurched, and
the lights turned warning red.

"This is Pursuit Probe Two," rasped
a slightly lower voice. "I am flying
alongside your ship. You have just

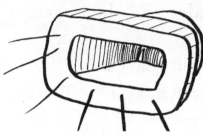 been hit by a
warning shot."

"If you do not
surrender, we
will open fire on
the count of three," said the first pursuit
probe. "One . . . two . . . "

Teggs shut his eyes tight as twin
explosions shuddered through the ship
and slammed him to the floor . . .

Chapter Six

CARNAGE IN SPACE

"Pursuit probes destroyed," said the computer calmly.

"What?" Teggs raised his head from the floor and opened his eyes. "But how? You said this ship wasn't armed!"

"This ship is not," the computer agreed. "But *that* one is."

Teggs looked at the scanner screen. It showed a large, ugly vessel armed  with massive space cannons floating just ahead of them. A huge hatch was opening in its front to reveal darkness beyond — and it was getting closer.

"Unknown craft has activated space magnet," said the computer. "It is dragging us inside."

"That's right, Teggs," snarled a low, gruff voice. "I'm taking you in!"

Teggs recognized the voice at once. "Tonka the mammoth! So this is a FANG ship!"

"Correct." Tonka's leering face appeared on the scanner. "You were doing such a rubbish job of escaping, I came to give you some help." His eyes glinted. "We don't want anything to happen to the Mega-Spray Y, do we?"

"Just what is this Mega-Spray Y?" Teggs demanded. "Why is it so important to the FANG?"

"That is our business," snapped Tonka. "Just bring it to my control room. There are other DSS ships coming and we must escape to Tartara at once."

Teggs scowled
as he picked
up the white
case. He
hated taking
orders from
a crooked
mammoth.
Reluctantly,
he stomped out of
Dutch's spaceship and
into the mammoth's dark, smelly vessel.
A lot of the corridors had been left
unfinished, and hundreds of half-drunk
mugs of tea littered the floor.

Following his nose, he found Tonka
in the control room. The big, brutish
mammoth's eyes lit up at the sight of
the white case. Then a loud beep
sounded.

"That's my space phone," Tonka
realized, pulling a metal cylinder from
his work belt.

"Tonka, this is FANG HQ." Attila's voice came hissing out of the phone. "A large DSS spaceship is coming your way. They might have seen you pick up Teggs. Change direction quickly—"

But Attila's warning had come too late. "Unmarked vessel, this is the DSS *Herbivore*," came a prim female voice over the ship's speakers. "We suspect you of destroying two pursuit probes and helping a criminal escape."

"Hang on," muttered Teggs. "She sounds familiar . . ."

Tonka ignored him and switched on his scanner. A large, pink, egg-shaped ship was approaching fast. The mammoth cursed and crossed to the ship's communicator. "Fair enough, *Herbivore*. You have caught me red-handed and red-trunked too. I give up."

Teggs stared at him. "You do?"

Tonka turned off the communicator and chuckled. "As if!" He curled his trunk around a big lever. "But now she thinks I've surrendered, she won't be expecting me to fire my *death lasers*!"

"No!" Teggs shouted. "You can't do that!"

"Wanna bet?" Tonka snarled. "I used to be known as Tonka the Traitor – even by my mum!"

Teggs dived towards him, but was too late. The mammoth yanked down on the lever. Instantly, bright green laser rays scorched through space and struck the *Herbivore*. A huge hole was blasted open and the pink ship sagged to one side.

"You double-crossing sack of slimy wool!" yelled Teggs in fury. He shoved the mammoth away from the lever and raised his spiky tail. "You will never hurt anyone else again!"

"Wrong!" said Tonka, whacking Teggs with his hairy trunk. "And if you take just one step closer, my friends at FANG HQ will blow up that bugging device on your shoulder!"

Teggs held the white case up against his neck and shook his head. "If they do, they'll blow up the Mega-Spray Y as well!"

"Stop arguing, you fools!" King Albu's voice squawked over Tonka's space phone. "The DSS *Herbivore* is fighting back!"

Both Teggs and Tonka swung round to face the scanner – and found five dung torpedoes streaking towards them . . .

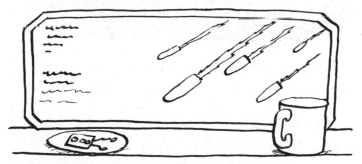

"Steer us away, you mammoth maniac!" Teggs shouted. "If that many missiles hit us head on– "

But even as he spoke, the dung torpedoes smashed into the ship and a stupendously smelly explosion tore through the control room. Tonka and Teggs were blown through the air as everything went black.

Teggs woke up aching all over. He was in a clean, pink room – with bars on the door. He tried to get to his feet, but found himself strapped to a stretcher. His dinner suit was reduced to rags, and his body was covered in  stinky soot from the explosion.

"Where am I?" he croaked.

"You are now on board the DSS *Herbivore*," came the prim voice he had heard before. "The same ship you tried to blow up after you 'surrendered' – you sneak! Luckily the damage isn't too bad . . ."

"I didn't fire at you," Teggs protested. He noticed a clock on the wall — and gasped as he realized he had just five hours to get back to Tartara. "Where's the Mega-Spray Y?" he asked desperately. "I need it!"

"Yes, I'm sure you do — *thief*!"

Teggs blinked as someone stepped forward to stand over him. She was a red, freckle-faced dinosaur with two sharp horns and a very cross expression on her pretty face. He recognized her at once — Damona the diceratops, his friendly (but quite annoying) rival from Astrosaurs Academy!

"It's you!" Teggs smiled weakly. "I *thought* your voice was familiar."

"Yes, it's me," said Damona, not smiling back. "I was looking forward to seeing you at the big academy reunion. But instead I had to leave it early and join the hunt for you!" She frowned. "My crew crossed to your ship and found you were knocked out. They brought you back here."

"It wasn't my ship," Teggs told her. "It belongs to a mammoth. Did your crew find him on board?"

"No," Damona informed him coldly. "Only you."

"He . . . he must have been hiding," Teggs realized.

"A likely story," said Damona. She looked at him and then the words burst out of her. "Oh, Teggs, how could you have turned into a criminal?"

I'm not a criminal! Teggs wanted to yell. But he knew that the FANG were listening to every word he said . . .

"Wait a second," said Damona. Teggs saw that she was staring at his shoulder through his ripped jacket. "What's that little disc there? Some sort of weird space gadget . . . ?"

"Nothing," Teggs insisted. He knew that if anyone tried to take off the bug, it would explode. "It's – it's just a badge."

Damona leaned over and plucked at it. "Don't lie to me! It's stuck to your skin." Teggs tried to twist away as she tugged at the disc again but the straps held him tight. "Let me see what it is."

"No, Damona, don't take it off!" Teggs struggled to break free with all his strength. "If you do, it's the end for us both – and Blink and Dutch too!"

Chapter Seven

THE DEADLY INTRUDER

"What *are* you on about, Teggs?"
Damona ripped the scorched and
dented disc free from his skin and held
it up to him. "Whatever this thing is,
it's totally broken."

"Broken?" Teggs opened one eye a
crack, then gave a long sigh of relief.

"It must have been splatted in the explosion . . . which means I can tell you what's been happening without the FANG knowing!"

"*Fang?*" said Damona, baffled. "And why did you mention Blink and Dutch?"

Teggs sighed. "You didn't see them at the academy reunion, did you?" She shook her head, and he continued: "That's because they've been taken prisoner by the Fearsome Army of Nasty Geniuses – the FANG – four of my deadliest enemies. I *had* to steal the Mega-Spray Y to save Blink and Dutch from being squished!"

Damona didn't look convinced. "You're making it up."

"I'm not!" Teggs insisted. Then a loud beep sounded close beside them. "That's Tonka's space phone!"

"My crew found it lying on the floor beside you." Damona fished the phone out of her pocket and it beeped again. "They thought it was yours."

"It must have been blown there by the explosion." Teggs looked at her desperately. "Damona, I know we didn't always get on at Astrosaurs Academy, but please . . . you *have* to trust me now." The phone beeped a third time and Teggs finally broke free of the straps on the stretcher and sat up. "Let me answer that thing — it's the only way I can prove I'm telling the truth!"

Damona looked at him long and hard. Then she sighed and offered him the space phone. Teggs grabbed it and switched on the speakers. "Hello?"

A cold voice rasped: "Is that Captain Teggs?"

"Yes." Teggs raised his eyebrows. "Is that King Albu, Crool Dasta, or Attila the Atrocious speaking?"

"Attila," came the throaty growl. "What is happening? Where is Tonka?"

"I don't know," Teggs admitted. "His

ship was blown up – and the explosion broke your bugging device. I was taken to the DSS *Herbivore* along with the Mega-Spray Y, and luckily they left Tonka's phone with me."

"Remember, you must tell no one that the FANG forced you to steal the Mega-Spray Y," Attila hissed. "And if you do not bring it to us within five hours, Blink Fingawing and Dutch Delaney will be destroyed!" Damona gasped. Teggs hastily shushed her. "It's OK. I, er, have a plan to trick the captain and take over the DSS *Herbivore*. I will set a course for Tartara as soon as I can."

"You had better . . ." Attila hissed. "And don't forget, we are monitoring all DSS communications. Ask anyone for help, and your friends will regret it!"

The space phone went dead. Teggs passed it back to Damona. "Now do you understand?"

She nodded, her eyes wide. "I've heard of evil Attila and Dasta . . . but didn't I read that King Albu the oviraptor had been eaten by a star-dragon?"

"I saw it happen," said Teggs with a shudder. "When I found out he was still alive I got the shock of my life!"

"Oh, Teggs, you poor thing. What a horrible time you've had!" Damona patted his spiky back. "But things are looking up."

"Oh?" He blinked. "Why?"

"Because now you've got *me* on your side." Damona grinned cheekily. "And

everyone knows I'm the greatest astrosaur ever in the universe!"

"Only because you've told them so!" Teggs teased. "Thanks, Damona."

"Luckily I *didn't* tell Admiral Rosso I had found you. I wanted to hear your story for myself first. And now I've heard it – next stop Tartara!" Damona picked up the white case. "On the way I'll find you a spare uniform and give this Mega-Spray Y to my lab boys so we can find out what it actually does."

Teggs nodded thoughtfully. "Maybe then we'll learn why the FANG want it so badly . . ."

Not far away, the *Sauropod* was still hot on the trail of Captain Teggs.

A red light started flashing on Gipsy's controls, and she turned to Arx. "Urgent call from Admiral Rosso incoming!"

A dimorphodon banged a button and Rosso appeared on the scanner screen. The old barosaurus looked even more serious than usual.

"Any sign of Teggs, sir?" Arx asked.

"No, but I have two other pieces of news," said Rosso. "Firstly, we now know that he has stolen the only sample of Mega-Spray Y – a brand-new liquid designed to dissolve scrap metal and plastic completely, leaving no mess or pollution behind."

"That's a great idea," said Iggy. "Junkyards will be a thing of the past."

Arx frowned. "But such a spray could also be a deadly weapon. It could melt all kinds of technology to mush."

"Very true," Rosso agreed. "And 'deadly' describes my second piece of news: Attila the Atrocious has escaped from space prison!"

"*What?*" Gipsy"s head-crest flushed blue with alarm.

"It seems that some weeks ago he built a dino-droid of himself from bits of scrap and left it in his cell," Rosso went on. "The guards didn't notice the difference till today! Now they're checking all the other prisoners in case Attila sneaked anyone out with him."

"That measly meat-chomper!" said Iggy fiercely. "Hey, you don't think Attila's swapped Teggs with one of his dino-droids, do you?"

Gipsy sat up in her seat. "He might have something to do with the captain acting so strangely!" she agreed.

"Well, I've got two hundred ships looking for Teggs – perhaps they'll find Attila by accident!" Rosso sighed. "Let me know if anything turns up, Arx."

"I will, sir," Arx promised as a dimorphodon squawked in his ear.

"Actually, it seems there's a badly damaged ship up ahead, close to a pair of wrecked pursuit probes. We'll check it out."

"Action, at last!" Iggy cried. "I'll take a look in Shuttle Alpha."

"I'm coming with you," said Gipsy. The pair of them ran from the flight deck to the *Sauropod*'s shuttle bay. Iggy fired up the dung-burners, opened the bay doors, and started to take the shuttle out into space. But then Gipsy caught sight of a silvery shape streaking towards them.

"What's that?" she asked urgently.

"It looks like a space-lifeboat," said
Iggy. "It must have come from that
wrecked ship."

"It's heading straight for us!" Gipsy
cried. "Steer out of the way, Ig!"

Iggy grabbed the controls – but too
late! The space-lifeboat crashed into
the nose of the shuttle and knocked it
flying. Iggy and Gipsy were sent
tumbling as the shuttle smashed back
inside the *Sauropod*. It landed on its
back, dented and smoking.

"Gipsy," Iggy groaned, "are you OK?"

"Just about." She kicked the door open.
"Whoever's inside that space-lifeboat
must be driving without a licence!"

"Maybe it's the captain," said Iggy,
crossing his claws. "Perhaps he's hurt
and needs our help!" He closed the bay
doors, took Gipsy's hand and they
clambered outside . . .

Only to find a scorched, slimy and
slightly sooty mammoth standing in the
space-lifeboat – aiming a cement
shooter right at them!

"I don't believe it!" Iggy gasped. "It's
Tonka – leader of the mammoth
wrecking crew!"

"Long time no see," snarled the
mammoth. "Now, where's Captain
Teggs?"

"We don't know," Gipsy snapped.
"And we wouldn't tell you if we did.
Last time we tangled you almost
destroyed a whole planet – and the
Sauropod!"

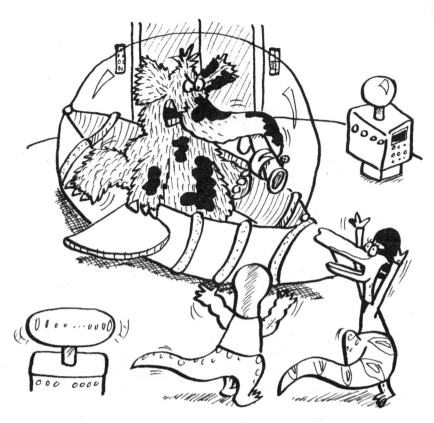

"Shut up," growled Tonka, waving the
weapon in their faces. "This time, I need
your ship. So lead me to the flight deck,
dino-fools – I'm taking over!"

Chapter Eight

PAINS, PLANS AND PERIL

Arx looked up as Gipsy and Iggy came gloomily back onto the flight deck. "You're back quickly," he said. "What did you find?"

"*Trouble!*" roared Tonka, just behind them. He shoved Iggy and Gipsy ahead of him, and the dimorphodon squawked and scattered.

"Tonka!" Arx jumped up from the control pit. "Where did *you* spring from?"

"Shut up and take this junk-heap to Tartara, right now!" said Tonka. "I don't know where Teggs has gone, but with you lot as my prisoners, he will soon be back under the FANG's control."

"The *FANG's* control?" Despite the danger of the situation, Arx felt a rush of hope. "Do you mean that you and this FANG have forced him to act like a criminal?"

"Er . . ." Tonka went cross-eyed. "Yes. Attila the Atrocious kidnapped his friends, Blink and Dutch – so he has to do as we say."

Gipsy gasped. "You mean Teggs *hasn't* gone bad?"

"I *knew* Attila had to be mixed up in this!" Iggy hooted with joy. "That's *brilliant!*"

"Oh, dear." Tonka scowled. "I – I wasn't supposed to tell you that."

"Mind in a muddle, is it?" Iggy looked at him closely. "Dear, oh dear – you're covered in oil too!"

"It's like you've swum in the stuff," Gipsy agreed.

"Sh-sh-shut up, both of you!" Tonka's hairy head was twitching. "Just g-g-g-get moving!" He shoved his cement shooter up against Arx's nose. "*NOW!*"

The *Sauropod* wasn't the only spaceship speeding towards Tartara. Damona's craft, the *Herbivore*, was getting closer all the time.

Teggs sat beside Damona on the flight deck, happier now he was back wearing an astrosaur uniform. "OK, FANG, open up," he said, speaking into the space phone. "I've locked away the *Herbivore*'s crew and brought you the Mega-Spray Y."

"You cut it fine, Teggs – you had
only one hour left," gurgled King Albu.
"We haven't got space in our base for
a ship that size. Take one of the
Herbivore's shuttles and come here at
once."

The large crater in the planet's
surface slid open to reveal the secret
tunnel beyond.

Teggs switched off the space phone
and turned to Damona. "OK, here's

the plan." He held up the white case. "I will do as they say and exchange this stuff for Blink and Dutch's freedom. As soon as the FANG opens the secret tunnel again to let us go—"

"I will zoom in and catch them all," Damona interrupted. "It's quite a good plan, I suppose. But what if they *don't* open the secret tunnel to let you out?"

"Then it was nice knowing you," said Teggs grimly.

"Goodbye, Teggs." Damona saluted him. Then she kissed him on the cheek. "That's for luck!"

Teggs pulled a face. "For *yuck*, more like!" Then he smiled. "See you soon – and stand by for action!"

With that, he ran off to the shuttle
bay and hopped into a small pink ship.
He took a deep breath. Then, as the bay
doors opened, Teggs zoomed off into
the blackness of the winding tunnel.

Soon he reached the parking bay.
Teggs jumped out with the white case.
The door in the wall was open, and he
walked through it warily.

It led into a dark and smelly control
room full of bones and bits of
technology. Big TV screens showed
amazing views of SSSS-One, the
Herbivore and surrounding space.
"Must be their monitoring system,"

Teggs muttered. Then his heart beat faster as he saw Blink and Dutch, still in chains, shuffle out of the gloom, prodded by Crool Dasta and Attila the Atrocious.

"Ah, Captain Eggs — I mean, Teggs!" said King Albu, pushing past his fellow FANGers. "Hand over the Mega-Spray Y."

"First things first," Teggs snapped, turning to Blink and Dutch. "Are you OK, guys?"

"We've been better," Blink admitted.

Dutch nodded. "I can't believe you're giving them that stuff, dude!"

"Neither can I." Teggs winked at him, then waved his white case at the three sinister carnivores. "I've done as you asked. Now set Blink and Dutch free and let us go."

"Very well," said Attila. "The Mega-Spray Y dissolves any metal. Use it now to remove your friends' chains."

Teggs frowned. "Er, what?"

"You heard," hissed Dasta. "It will be a useful demonstration of the invention."

"Yes, go on, Teggs," Blink urged him. "These chains weigh a ton!"

But still Teggs hesitated.

"*Do it!*" roared King Albu.

Teggs slowly
opened the
case and
pulled out
a spray
bottle.
Suddenly,
Attila did
a funky
disco leap and

snatched the spray away. Before Teggs
could stop him, he
had squirted a cloud of the stuff at
Blink and Dutch's chains . . .

And absolutely nothing happened.

"I knew it!" growled Attila, spraying
the air in front of him and tasting it
with his tongue. "This is *not* Mega-
Spray Y. It's *water*!"

"So . . ." Dasta's eyes narrowed. "You
tried to cheat us!"

"You stupid stegosaur!" King Albu
hopped up and down with rage. "Did

you really think you could trick the FANG with such a simple swap?"

"Well, I thought I'd have a go," Teggs confessed. "The real Mega-Spray Y is still on board the DSS *Herbivore*. I'll let you have it once Blink, Dutch and I are safely away from here."

"Another pitiful attempt to trick us!" roared Attila. "But your plans are doomed to fail, Teggs. Because you don't know where Tonka is right now, do you?"

"I don't much care either," Teggs retorted.

"You should!" King Albu pointed to the screens on the wall.

Teggs's heart leaped at the sight of his huge silver spaceship soaring into view. "The *Sauropod*!" he cried.

But then the view changed to show the ship's flight deck. And there, in the control pit, sat Tonka!

"I have taken charge of the *Sauropod*!" The mammoth's slightly mangled body rocked with laughter. "Arx, Iggy, Gipsy and your entire crew are my helpless prisoners."

Teggs felt his blood boil. "You haven't won yet!" he shouted at the screen. "I still have the real Mega-Spray Y!"

"Wanna bet?" Tonka held up a familiar-looking white spray can, and dragged someone else into view with his trunk – Damona!

"I'm sorry, Teggs," Damona wailed. "The *Sauropod* pulled up alongside my ship, and Tonka told me he would squish your entire crew if I didn't come on board with the Mega-Spray Y. Now he's got us all!"

Tonka laughed. "Open up the secret

tunnel, Attila, and I'll join you down there in a shuttle."

"Well done, my fellow FANG-fiend." Attila crossed to a control panel and pulled a big lever to open the sliding crater. "You have lost, Teggs!"

Teggs hung his head. "So it seems," he whispered.

Dasta hopped about with evil glee. "We have you, your friends, your ship *and* the invention you stole for us – all within our power."

"Our revenge is complete." King Albu threw back his ugly head and roared with laughter as the rest of the FANG joined in. "At last Teggs Stegosaur is utterly, totally and absolutely defeated!"

Chapter Nine

THE SECRET OF THE FANG

The FANG gang went on laughing
and crowing. Blink and Dutch stared
helplessly as Teggs sank to his knees
beside his white case, which was lying
all but forgotten on its side.

"You are right,"
Teggs muttered.
"I am hopelessly
beaten . . ."
But then
he reached
into the
case – and
pulled out
a ray gun!

"Or I *would* be if I hadn't planned ahead!" He jumped back up and trained the weapon on King Albu with a sharp little smile. "Now, I don't like guns, but I like *you* even less. So tell Tonka to give himself up or else I'll change the gun's setting from stun beam to laser – and blast you all to atomic pieces!"

"Way to go, dude!" Dutch cheered, and Blink beamed and clapped his chained-up wings.

"You want to shoot?" snarled King Albu. "Go ahead!"

"Eh?" Teggs frowned. "You might have come back from the dead once, but don't push your luck!"

"We cannot die, Teggs." Dasta scuttled towards him and smiled. "Because we were never alive . . ."

Suddenly, his eyes turned red and began to spin around – and so did King Albu's! Blink twittered in fright while Dutch gasped in amazement.

Without warning, a small metal tube slid out of Albu's forehead and shot bullets of light at Teggs's hand. Teggs yelped as the gun was blasted from his grip.

"I should have realized," he groaned, rubbing his sore hand. "They're not the *real* King Albu and Crool Dasta at all – and I bet Tonka is just a trick too. They are all robotic *dino-droids*, built by Attila!"

"At last, the orange oaf understands!" Attila performed a sinister boogie. "The real Tonka and Dasta are still locked up in my old space prison. You suspected your *friends* might be dino-droids, but never my evil allies."

"You almost messed up when you chose King Albu, though, didn't you?" Teggs said. "You didn't know that I saw him squished with my own eyes!"

"True. I *really* wanted to make a dino-droid of General Loki," Attila confided. "But you have fought him so often, you might have guessed he was a fake." He sighed. "Besides, I couldn't find the right coloured paint! I had to work quickly before my escape from prison was discovered. Like this underground base, Dasta, Albu and Tonka were made in a rush. They are not quite perfect . . . but they have served their purpose."

Teggs scowled. "They certainly tricked me."

"Don't feel too bad, Teggs," said Attila mockingly. "Worried for your academy friends, cut off from your crew and rattled by so many old enemies, you couldn't think straight – just as I planned!"

"Now I understand why you wanted the Mega-Spray Y so badly," Blink realized. "That stuff would dissolve a metal-and-plastic dino-droid in moments."

Dutch nodded. "But now you've got some, you can find a way to protect your robot things from being mashed!"

Attila nodded eagerly. "Then nothing in the universe will be able to so much as scratch my creations. I shall replace all living dinosaurs with everlasting robots . . . and they will obey only *me*!" He chuckled. "I think I shall start by replacing the three of you. Albu, Dasta – *destroy them*!"

Their eyes still spinning and glowing red, the mechanical carnivores began to advance . . .

Striding forward
fearlessly, Teggs
whacked the
Dasta-droid
with his
tail and
sent him
staggering.
But the fake
Albu let rip
with more super-bright bullets
from his forehead
and blasted
Teggs to the
floor. Attila
cheered as
the two dino-
droids bore
down on the
stegosaurus,
their gleaming
claws reaching
for his throat . . .

But suddenly, with a fierce roar,
Dutch broke free of his chains and
smashed both dino-droids aside with
his powerful tail.

"Impossible!" cried Attila. "You are
not strong enough to have broken your
bonds!"

"True, dude," Dutch agreed. "But
while you were busy yakking, Blink
grabbed that ray gun Teggs threw our
way and *blasted* through my chains!"

Blink beamed. "And guess what." He spread his large, leathery wings and his own chains fell away. "I've just freed myself as well!"

Teggs struggled up as Blink quickly tossed him the ray gun. "And while the stun ray won't work on your robot-pets, it can still take care of you!"

"First, you have to hit me," squealed Attila, dodging two shots from Teggs as he dived behind a control panel. "Before my dino-droids destroy you all!"

With horror, Teggs saw that Albu and Dasta were already back on their robotic feet and lumbering towards him. "And not just those two," growled Attila, hitting some switches. "Let us see how you fare against my early test versions. Not as convincing in the 'look-alike' stakes – but just as deadly!"

A sliding door opened and ten more robotic terrors jerked menacingly into the room – there were three different Albus, three Dastas and four very threatening Tonkas. The faces were half finished and scary. Their crimson eyes spun like Catherine wheels. Shiny metal muscles replaced green scales or straggly wool, and missiles and laser guns were already emerging from holes in their heads and arms.

"Er, dudes?" said Dutch nervously.
"Remember back at the academy we
used to call ourselves the Daring
Dinos?"

Blink gulped and nodded. "Now
we've got to *really* live up to that
name!"

"Right!" Teggs gave them a brave
grin and held out his right hand. "Do
we dare?"

Dutch and Blink put their hands on
his and smiled back. "*WE DARE!*"

114

And with a loud whoop, the three
old friends joined together in battle
once more!

Blink launched himself into the air.
Two of the Dasta-droids fired missiles
from their heads, but he spun about to
avoid them.

As explosions went off all around
him, Teggs performed a spiky eight-ton
cartwheel and knocked two of the
metal mammoths flying.

Dutch dodged a laser beam and
swatted an Albu-droid
with his long neck.
Then he tripped up
two Tonkas with his
tail and squashed a
Dasta-droid with his
big, scaly bottom.
But suddenly, one
of the King Albus shot
bolts of electricity from his
claws into the metal floor.

Teggs and Dutch gasped and shook
with pain as electric shocks flashed
through them. Blink swooped down
and tried to lift the two of them
clear of the sparking floor, but he
got shocked too. All three astrosaurs
collapsed in a heap.

The shocks stopped at last, and Teggs
opened his eyes – to find the twelve
dino-droids stomping towards him and
his friends. "Come on," he gasped,
dragging Blink and Dutch to their feet.
"Maybe we can shelter in Damona's
shuttle—"

"I don't think so," said a gruff mammoth voice from the parking-bay doorway.

Teggs swung round to find the way to the bay blocked by a scorched and oily Tonka – leading Arx, Iggy, Gipsy and Damona behind him in chains.

"Guys!" cried Teggs. "Are you OK?"

"Sorry we tried to stop you before, Captain," said Arx. He and the other astrosaurs looked very downcast. "And sorry we've let you down now."

"Forget it," Teggs murmured. "I know you did your best. No one can ask for more."

"I certainly can't!" cried Attila, jumping out from hiding and boogieing with delight. "It's over, Teggs. Now my mechanical pets shall deal with you – slowly . . ."

Teggs clutched hold of Dutch and Blink as the twelve deadly dino-droids closed in for the kill.

Chapter Ten

SPRAY IT AGAIN!

As the murderous machines stalked closer and closer, Iggy cleared his throat. "Er, excuse me, Attila,"  he said, patting the mammoth beside him. "But now all the dino-droids are together, I think Tonka here would like to say something."

The mangled mammoth lifted his trunk and strode forward.

"Say something, Ig?" Gipsy grinned and shook her head. "I think you mean . . . *Spray* something!"

At her command, using his trunk like
a hosepipe, the fake Tonka sprayed
brown, smelly liquid all over the place!

"Duck, Teggs!" Damona shouted.

Teggs did as she said, dragging Blink
and Dutch down with him. The dino-
droids were drenched in the dirty
downpour . . .

And suddenly, they started to melt!

"*Nooooooooo!*" bellowed Attila in
helpless rage – just as Arx, Gipsy, Iggy
and Damona all threw off their chains!

"We're not really prisoners." Arx
beamed. "Tricky Tonka here *tried* to
take over the *Sauropod*—"

"But he was damaged when
Damona blew up his ship," said Gipsy
breathlessly. "He started going wrong."

"He was leaking oil," Iggy agreed.
"And up close I could hear his circuits
whirring! Knowing Attila was on the
loose, I guessed that Tonka must be a
dino-droid."

"So together we overpowered him," Arx explained. "Then Iggy was able to rewire his computer brain and make him work for *us*!"

Teggs watched as the mammoth spat more of the mucky liquid and dissolved a bank of controls. "And that's not just any old spray, is it?" He grinned at his crew. "It's the real Mega-Spray Y!"

Damona nodded. "When I saw the *Sauropod* approaching Tartara, I went over in a shuttle and told Arx what was happening. We shoved a spray can inside Tonka's mechanical trunk, and tricked the FANG into thinking we were their prisoners . . ."

"Awesome!" Dutch cheered.

"Now let's polish off these melting monsters," said Gipsy. "Together!" And with a fierce yell, she hoof-jabbed the nearest Albu-droid and whacked its metal head clear off!

"I like your style, Gipsy!" cried Damona. And as one of the phoney Tonkas tried to fire its lasers at Teggs, she rammed it with her horns and smashed it to soggy pieces.

Meanwhile, Arx and Iggy wasted no time demolishing three dissolving Dastas. "It's very satisfying to crunch that crummy carnivore three times over!" Iggy remarked.

"You know it, dude!" shouted Dutch, as he and Blink took care of a pair of melting Albu-droids.

"Captain!" Gipsy pointed as she trashed a Tonka-droid with her tail. "Attila's getting away!"

Punching the most dangerous Dasta-droid into techno-trickles, Teggs saw the evil genius running for the back way out. "Oi, Attila!" he yelled. "You forgot to pack your *trunk*!"

So saying, he wrenched off the tame Tonka's woolly trunk – still loaded with Mega-Spray Y – and hurled it across the control room. It hit Attila on the head and drenched him.

"You stego-dunce!" bawled Attila, still running. "I am not made of metal! The spray does not work on me— *Whoops!*"

His silver shorts fell down around his ankles and tripped him up! He went flying head-over-heels, crashed into the wall and lay still with his bottom poking up in the air.

"Good thinking, Captain!" Iggy grinned. "Attila might not have been made of metal – but his belt buckle *was*!"

"I'm just glad he was wearing underpants." Gipsy shuddered. "Yuck!"

"Both he *and* his pants will soon be back in prison," said Arx, staring round at twelve pools of sludgy goo – all that was left of the dissolved dino-droids.

Even the tame, trunkless techno-Tonka was now little more than a sticky bundle of rotten wool.

"Let's hope that's the last we hear of Attila *and* the FANG," said Teggs with feeling. "His plans are ruined — just like his robots."

"But our big reunion has been ruined too," said Blink sadly.

"Come off it, beak-face," said Damona, slapping him on the back. "Being back in action together is the best reunion of all!"

Dutch grabbed her in a jokey headlock. "You may be right there!"

Meanwhile, Arx and Gipsy had crossed over to one of Attila's control panels and were flicking some switches.

"Hey, what are you two up to?" Iggy wondered.

The next moment he had his answer, as Admiral Rosso's face appeared on one of the big screens on the wall. "Yes? Who's calling?"

"Only us, sir," said Arx happily. "We couldn't wait to tell you *three* bits of great news."

Gipsy nodded. "We've caught Attila, we've got back the Mega-Spray Y – and best of all, we've found out that Captain Teggs isn't a crook at all."

"He was made to steal that stuff against his will!" squawked Blink.

"He's the same hero he always was," added Dutch proudly.

A huge grin spread over Rosso's wrinkly face. "I knew Teggs couldn't *really* be a criminal! I'll call off the hunt for him at once."

Teggs crossed to the screen and saluted. "Thanks, sir. I'm just sorry I couldn't tell you what was going on sooner." He beamed. "Though if it wasn't for the bravery of my very best friends — past *and* present — I wouldn't be standing here to tell you now!"

"Well, explanations can wait," said Rosso. "I'll arrange a big party for you all at DSS HQ. Everyone must come along at once. You can drop Attila back in space prison on the way!"

"Will do, sir," Teggs promised. "See you soon."

As Rosso's face faded from the screen, Dutch walked up to Teggs and shook his hand. "You risked a lot for us, dude. Thanks."

Teggs blushed. "That's what friends are for."

Blink nodded quickly and shook his other hand. "You're not just a brilliant friend – you're the greatest astrosaur in the universe!"

"Apart from me of course," said Damona, smiling as everyone groaned.

Gipsy ran over to Teggs and gave him a massive hug. "I'm so glad to have you back, Captain!"

"I'm just sorry I had to push past you all like that on SSSS-One," said Teggs.

"Oh, forget it," said Iggy, hugging them both. "Everything's back to normal, and I'm going to party all night long!"

"Me too!" Arx did a little jig, and Dutch and Blink joined in.

"You know, Teggs, you really do have an amazing crew," said Damona.

"Could I borrow them for my own missions from time to time?"

"Sorry, Damona," said Teggs, "but I wouldn't swap Arx, Gipsy and Iggy for anything in the universe. We'll soon be sinking our teeth into another exciting adventure . . ." He bounded over to Attila and lifted him by the tail. "Because the FANG's been sunk for good!"

THE END